# The Shopping Basket
## *John Burningham*

Thomas Y. Crowell    New York

Other books by John Burningham

MR. GUMPY'S MOTOR CAR
COME AWAY FROM THE WATER, SHIRLEY
TIME TO GET OUT OF THE BATH, SHIRLEY
WOULD YOU RATHER…

Little Books

THE BABY
THE BLANKET
THE CUPBOARD
THE DOG
THE FRIEND
THE RABBIT
THE SCHOOL
THE SNOW

Library of Congress Catalog Card Number: 80-7987
Copyright © 1980 by John Burningham
First published in Great Britain by Jonathan Cape Ltd
All rights reserved
Layout and design Jan Pienkowski

ISBN 0–690–04082–2 (tr)
ISBN 0–690–04083–0 (lb)

Printed in Italy by New Interlitho SpA, Milan

"Go down to the store for me, will you,
Steven, and buy six eggs, five bananas, four
apples, three oranges for the baby, two
doughnuts and a package of crisps for your lunch.
And leave this note at number 25."

So Steven set off for the store, carrying his basket.
He passed number 25,

the gap in the railings,

the full litter basket,

the men digging up the pavement

and the house where the nasty dog lived,

and arrived at the store.

He bought the six eggs, five bananas, four apples, three oranges for the baby, two doughnuts and a package of crisps for his lunch. But when he came out of the store there was a bear.

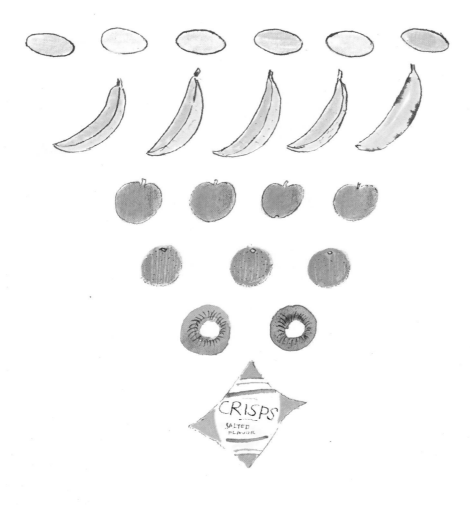

"I want those eggs," said the bear, "and if you don't give them to me I will hug all the breath out of you."

"If I threw an egg up in the air," said Steven, "you are so slow I bet you couldn't even catch it."

"Me slow!" said the bear…

And Steven hurried on home carrying his basket.
But when he got to the house where the nasty
dog lived there was a monkey.

"Give me those bananas," said the monkey, "or I'll pull your hair."

"If I threw a banana on to that kennel, you're so noisy I bet you couldn't get it without waking the dog."

"Me noisy!" said the monkey…

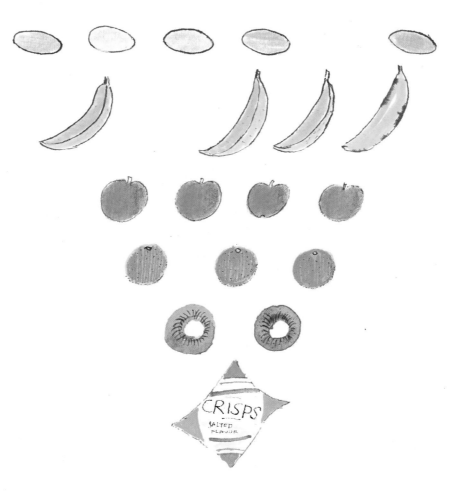

So Steven hurried on home carrying his basket.
But when he got to where the men were
digging up the pavement there was
a kangaroo.

"Give me those apples you have in your basket," said the kangaroo, "or I'll thump you."

"If I threw an apple over that tent, you're so clumsy I bet you couldn't even jump over to get it."

"Me clumsy!" said the kangaroo...

And Steven hurried on home carrying his basket.
But when he got to the litter basket
there was a goat.

"Give me the oranges you have in your basket," said the goat, "or I'll butt you over the fence."

"If I put an orange in that litter basket, you're so stupid I bet you couldn't even get it out."

"Me stupid!" said the goat...

So Steven hurried on home carrying his basket.
But when he got to the gap in the railings
there was a pig.

"Give me those doughnuts," said the pig, "or I'll squash you against the railings."

   "If I put the doughnuts through that gap in the railings, you're so fat I bet you couldn't squeeze through and get them."

   "Me fat!" said the pig…

So Steven hurried on home carrying his basket.
But when he got to number 25 there was
an elephant.

"Give me those crisps," said the elephant, "or I'll whack you with my trunk."

"If I put these crisps through that letter box, your trunk is so short I bet you could not even reach it."

"My trunk short!" said the elephant...

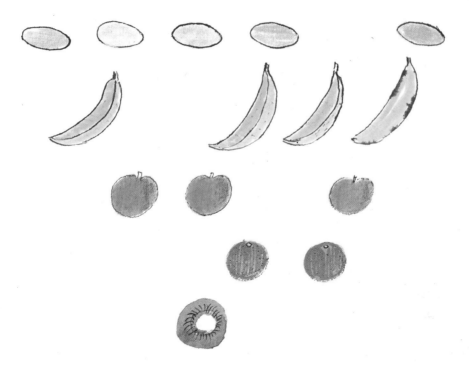

And Steven hurried on home carrying his basket.
But when he got to his own house, there was
his mother.

"Where on earth have you been, Steven? I only asked you to get six eggs, five bananas, four apples, three oranges, two doughnuts and a package of crisps. How could it have taken so long?"

E
BUR    Burningham, John
       The shopping basket

$12.89

DATE